Brian ran toward the fence.

He was going all out, seeming to keep up as the ball angled downward. He could get there if . . .

He remembered what had happened before and checked quickly to make sure he had room.

Just before he reached the fence he slowed, and then he jumped—stretched full out.

That fraction of a second seemed like a minute. . . .

*Look for these books about the
Angel Park All-Stars*

WHAT A CATCH!

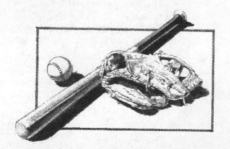

By Dean Hughes

Illustrated by Dennis Lyall

Bullseye Books • Alfred A. Knopf
New York

A BULLSEYE BOOK PUBLISHED BY ALFRED A. KNOPF, INC.
Copyright © 1990 by Dean Hughes
Cover art copyright © 1990 by Rick Ormond
Interior illustrations copyright © 1990 by Dennis Lyall
ANGEL PARK ALL-STARS characters copyright © 1989 by
Alfred A. Knopf, Inc.
Bullseye Books and Angel Park All-Stars are trademarks
of Alfred A. Knopf, Inc.

Library of Congress Cataloging-in-Publication Data
Hughes, Dean, 1943–
What a catch! / by Dean Hughes.
p.   cm.—(Angel Park all-stars ; 4)
Summary: Brian Waters is so nervous that he can't seem to do
anything right on his little league team, the Angel Park Dodgers,
but a pep talk from a big league star psyches him up to make a
winning catch.
ISBN 0-679-90429-8 (lib. bdg.) — ISBN 0-679-80429-3 (pbk.)
[1. Baseball—Fiction.   2. Self-confidence—Fiction.]   I. Title.
II. Series: Hughes, Dean, 1943–Angel Park all-stars ; 4.
PZ7.H87312Wh   1990
[Fic]—dc20   89-28876
CIP
AC

RL: 2:7
First Bullseye Books edition: June 1990
Manufactured in the United States of America
1 2 3 4 5 6 7 8 9 10

for Jonathan Hughes

★1★

Goose Egg

═══════════════════════

"Move back, Brian!" Coach Wilkens yelled.

Brian walked back several steps toward the right field fence and got ready. He saw the Tigers' batter take a big swing. When he heard the *crack!* he took off.

The ball arched high, and Brian kept his eye on it as he ran hard—straight away from the plate. It was way back, but he had a chance.

He was getting there.

He could do it.

He reached up . . . stretched, and . . . *crash!!!!!*

Brian saw flashes: stars and stripes and fireworks. For a few seconds he didn't know what had happened.

Then he remembered the feel of the chain-link fence as it bashed his shoulder and cheek.

And something had hit him right on the top of his head.

Brian reached up to rub it. . . .

And then he realized something was going on. He was lying on the grass. Where was the ball?

He jumped up and looked around. Sterling Malone, his teammate, had run all the way from center field. He scooped up the ball and made a hard throw back to the infield.

But it was too late. The runner had rounded third and was heading home.

The Dodgers were still way ahead, 9 to 2. But Brian could have held the hit to a double if he had checked to see how close the fence was. He knew he had made a stupid mistake.

"Are you okay?" Sterling asked.

Brian wasn't sure. He touched his cheek—which was bleeding a little—but it was the knock on the head that was hurting.

He was beginning to think he knew what had happened. "Did the ball . . . ?"

"It hit the fence and then bounced off your head," Sterling said.

"Yeah, that's what I thought."

"You didn't bust anything, did you?"

"I don't think so." Brian rubbed his arm and then rolled his shoulder around a couple of times.

"You gave it a good shot, Brian," Sterling said, smiling a little.

Brian didn't need that. Everyone would think it was a big joke. He could hear them now: "Dumb little Brian ran into the fence and let the ball bounce off his head."

Coach Wilkens was running toward Brian. He looked worried.

"I'm okay," Brian mumbled as the coach reached him.

"Where did the ball hit you?"

Brian didn't want to say.

"You better come and sit down."

So the coach took him out of the game.

Brian walked to the dugout and plunked himself down on the bench. Everyone was watching him, and he felt stupid. He was glad this was only a practice game. Not many people were in the bleachers.

The Dodgers' players tried to make Brian

feel better. They told him he had made a great try.

But the Tigers were yelling all sorts of cute remarks from the other dugout.

"Hey, right fielder, that's using your head!"

"This isn't soccer. You can catch it with your hands!"

And then someone in the bleachers bellowed, "Hey, Waters, did you think that was a shortcut to the bathroom?"

Brian ducked his head. He couldn't believe it. It must have been some player from one of the teams in his league. Everyone by now seemed to know about his . . . "problem."

Sometimes Brian got nervous.

And sometimes—when he got really nervous—he needed to go to the bathroom.

And sometimes that need got downright urgent.

He had made some desperate trips—during games—and once had barely made it back in time to bat. And now they had all started to tease him. Some guys called him "Running Waters."

But tonight Brian had no reason to be

nervous. This was just an extra tune-up before their big first-half championship game on Saturday. It should have been a night to relax.

"Don't pay attention to them," Billy Bacon, the Dodgers' catcher, told Brian. "Their guys stand in the outfield and pick their noses. They couldn't get to a ball hit that far."

But the Tigers weren't Brian's real worry. His problem was, he kept trying harder and harder, and he only seemed to mess up more.

As he had walked into the dugout he'd heard the Dodgers' star pitcher, Rodney Bunson, say, "Brian's playing worse all the time."

And Brian knew that was true.

How could he have let the ball bounce off his head?

He had made some real bonehead plays lately, but this was the worst yet.

He rubbed his head. He was getting a goose egg. Lately that's what he had been getting when he batted, too—lots of big goose eggs.

And now he had to sit on the bench.

The Dodgers were at bat again, and Kenny Sandoval came over and sat down next to Brian. He was the rookie star on the Little League team. He was only nine, a third-grader, but he was big for his age—and *really* good. Kenny didn't say anything.

Henry White grounded out to open the inning, and Eddie Boschi struck out. But Kenny was next, and *smack,* he hit a clean line drive for a base hit.

Kenny made baseball look easy. Brian wondered how he did it.

Rodney Bunson followed with a double, and Sterling Malone walked. What had looked like a bad inning was turning around. A few more runs would put the game on ice.

It was the third inning, and the coach was starting to substitute. "Harlan, bat for Jenny," he called over to the dugout.

Harlan Sloan walked out and got a bat. Brian found himself wishing that someone besides Harlan could drive these runs in.

Harlan slashed a grounder that shot under the shortstop's glove and into left. Kenny scored.

Brian watched Harlan grin from first base. Kenny clapped his hands and yelled, "Way to go, Harlan!"

Harlan was another third-grader—another rookie—and the worst player on the team. But he was getting better every game. Brian knew he should be happy for him—but it wasn't easy. He didn't want to lose his starting position to one of those little kids.

It wasn't easy, either, when Jacob Scott, the other rookie on the team, also got a hit and scored a run. Jacob was in the game for Brian. And Brian was on the bench because of that stupid play.

Even Eddie Boschi pitched a good game. He was a pretty good player, though only the third-best pitcher, and sometimes he had his problems. But he was improving, too.

Maybe everyone was—except Brian.

If only he could have made that catch. . . .

Big Star

The next day Kenny called Brian to invite him for some extra practice. Just the third-graders—and Brian.

Brian wasn't sure he liked that. He may have been small, but he was no rookie. All the same, he said he would meet the guys at the park. It was something to do.

He found his glove in the corner—where he had thrown it in disgust after the game the night before. One thing he knew for sure: He *did* need some extra practice.

Maybe some of the other players would show up and he wouldn't be stuck with only the rookies.

But when Brian got to the park he saw

just the three third-graders. He was probably the only older guy they felt sorry
for.

Kenny walked up to him and said, "I'll
hit some fly balls to you guys, if you want."

"Is that what you think I need to work
on?" Brian asked.

Kenny shrugged. "We all do, Brian."

It was hard to be mad at Kenny. Brian
knew he was only trying to help.

So Brian trotted to the outfield with
Jacob and Harlan.

And he showed the third-grade rookies
what a sixth-grader could do. He made all
the tough catches. He amazed *himself* a couple of times.

Why couldn't he catch the ball like that
during the games?

When Kenny really slammed one, Brian
went flying back, reached up, and snagged
the ball in the webbing of his glove.

"Wow!" Jacob yelled. *"What a catch!"*

Brian knew it had been good, and he liked
to see the rookies impressed, but he acted
as though it was no big deal.

The boys traded places soon after that,

and Jacob did the hitting. Kenny made a nice catch, and Brian said, "Good catch, Kenny."

Kenny threw the ball back and then walked closer to Brian. "Brian, don't you think you're just getting too uptight in the games? You play great out here."

"I know," Brian said. And then he surprised himself by adding, "It seems like the harder I try, the worse I get."

Kenny nodded. "Yeah, that's what happened to me for a few games."

But Kenny didn't know how much worse it was for Brian.

Brian had been the smallest one in his class all the way through school. All the kids teased him about it. Brian wanted to prove that he was really good at something—no matter how little he was.

Just then a car pulled up to the curb at the edge of the park. Brian recognized Kenny's dad. Mr. Sandoval got out of the car, and so did another man.

Mr. Sandoval waved and shouted, "Come here!"

Kenny started toward the car, but his dad

yelled, "All of you. I want you to meet someone."

As all the boys walked to the car, Brian lagged behind a little. He didn't know why the other three suddenly came to a stop. He heard Jacob say, "I don't *believe* it."

"Come on over," Kenny's dad said. "Don't you want to meet Gary Gentel?"

Brian stopped, too.

Like a statue.

Gary Gentel?

The star of the L.A. Dodgers? *That* Gary Gentel?

It couldn't be.

The guy stepped forward, grinning.

It was him. Same big jaw. Same unshaven face. But he didn't look quite as tough as he did on TV.

"I don't *believe* it!" Jacob said again—for about the tenth time.

The boys were hurrying toward him now.

"I ran into him at the mall in San Lorenzo," Mr. Sandoval said. "He was signing autographs. So I invited him over to meet Kenny . . . and the rest of you."

What? Brian thought. How could he do that?

"We're old friends," Kenny's dad went on. "We played Triple-A ball together. If you guys want to come with us, we'll go get a Coke or something. He's only got about an hour before he has to head to the stadium."

The boys were all saying, "Yeah, sure," as they lined up to shake hands.

"Can we get your autograph?" Harlan asked.

"Sure," Gentel said, and he slapped Harlan on the shoulder. "So you guys are all playing your first year, I understand."

He shook hands with Brian.

Brian was embarrassed. "No. *They* are. I'm twelve. This is my fourth year."

"Oh. I see. You're sort of . . ." Gentel stopped just before the word "small." Brian could see that he was embarrassed, too. "How did you bang up your face?"

That's the last thing Brian wanted to talk about.

"He almost made a great play last night," Mr. Sandoval said. "He ran into the fence trying to catch a fly ball."

"Hey, now that's the kind of play I like," Gentel said. "I like to see a guy go all out like that."

Yeah, and let the ball bounce off his head?

But Brian didn't say that. He just nodded.

Jacob was crowding in closer. "Mr. Gentel, before we leave, do you think you could teach us some stuff—maybe give us some pointers?"

Jacob's normally loud voice was suddenly barely a whisper. He started mumbling, "I know your batting average for every year of your career. I know *everything* about you. I even have a poster of you on my wall."

Gentel laughed. "Yeah, I'll give you some pointers. What do you need to work on most?"

"Ground balls," Harlan said before Jacob could answer.

"All right. Let's go back out on the infield, and I'll hit you some grounders. We'll talk about some of the basics."

And so the boys went back to the field, and the star hit ground balls to them. It was too much to believe. And it was scary.

"Come toward the ball. Play the ball—don't let the ball play you," he coached them.

"That's it. Keep the ball in front of you. Watch it all the way into your glove."

Then to Harlan: "Get down lower. Don't bend so much at the waist. Bend your knees. Keep your elbows loose."

Brian was almost sick. He just knew he was going to mess up. And he did.

He let the ball come up on him and bounce off his chest.

"Relax," Gentel yelled. "Just watch the ball. Stay down and pick it up. It's not hard if you don't let the ball scare you."

But Brian was just as bad the next time. He was all stiff and awkward.

As he waited his next turn he fidgeted nervously. His old problem was coming back.

This time he bent down with straight arms, and *zip,* the ball shot right between his legs. He couldn't believe it.

Gentel shouted, "Brian, you're standing stiff and letting the ball come at you. You need to come forward and get low." He showed Brian the motion.

But Brian knew the motion. He just couldn't do it right now. He was shaking all over.

And besides, his situation was getting urgent. Suddenly he knew he couldn't wait. "Excuse me," he said, and he took off toward the park men's room.

He felt like the biggest idiot in the world. No.

The *smallest* idiot in the world.

And by the time he came out of the men's room he couldn't face going back. He ran all the way home—the long way—so he wouldn't have to look Gary Gentel in the eye ever again.

★ 3 ★

Taking Heat

When Brian got home he pulled the plug on his phone, and he stayed in his room all evening.

He had his own private phone and his own TV. He had just about everything. His family was as well off as almost anyone in Angel Park. But right then he would have given everything he had to be Kenny Sandoval instead of Brian Waters.

Or worse, *Running* Waters!

What if the rookies told everyone what had happened? How could he face that?

Maybe he should just quit the team.

But deep down, he knew he couldn't give

up baseball. He just had to do better in the game tomorrow—and face the teasing.

That was nothing new.

But he wouldn't drink a drop of water all day. In fact, he would stop drinking right now. Never again was he going to take off in the middle of a game.

The game was with the San Lorenzo Mariners—a team the Dodgers should be able to beat without much trouble. Brian thought it might be his chance to look good.

On Wednesday afternoon he showed up early. He concentrated during pregame batting practice—and did well. He ran hard when the coach hit fly balls, and he made some good catches, too.

But the day was extremely hot, and Brian was nervous. He kept wiping the sweat from his face, and he felt sort of weak before the game even started.

The coach told the players not to look past the Mariners. "I know the big game is on Saturday. But right now *this* is the one to worry about. Let's play like it's for the championship."

And then he announced the starting lineup.

Brian had to wait all the way to the end. But he was batting ninth and starting in right field.

He took a deep breath of relief. He had half expected to be on the bench.

As the players walked away Kenny said, "Just have fun today, Brian. You'll do okay."

And Brian believed he would do better. At least he wouldn't have to go to the bathroom!

Brian thought he would never mention what had happened at the park, but he found himself asking, "What did Gary Gentel say?"

"About what?"

"About me taking off."

"My dad told him you were probably embarrassed. He said you're a really good player, but you get nervous."

"What did you guys do?"

"We went and got a root beer at the A & W."

"Was Gary Gentel pretty cool?"

"Yeah. He told some funny stories about

my dad. And Jacob asked him about a thousand questions."

Brian was *very* jealous, but he wouldn't have admitted it for anything.

The Dodgers batted first, but they didn't score.

Kenny struck out two batters in the bottom of the first, and the ball never came Brian's way. He was relieved. But he did want to make some good plays before the game was over.

In the second inning Brian came up to bat with Billy Bacon on base and one run in. It was a chance to start building a good lead—and a chance for Brian to break out of his batting slump.

But Brian swung at a pitch way inside.

The ball hit off the bat handle with a *thud* and rolled toward first.

Brian knew the pitcher would have to hurry, so he turned on his speed and made the play close.

But just as he stretched for the bag he heard the ball pop into the first baseman's glove.

"Out!!!!!" the umpire yelled.

The score stayed 1 to 0 for the Dodgers.

And Brian felt he had let his team down again.

In the bottom of the inning Kenny got the first batter out on a pop-up, but the Mariners' little shortstop hit a slow roller to third that made Henry White hurry. His throw was wide. Jenny Roper was lucky even to get a glove on it and hold the runner at first.

"Everyone makes mistakes," Brian told himself. "Henry's the best third baseman in the league, and he just messed up."

But he was still worried what he might do if a ball was hit to him. He took off his hat and wiped his face with his sleeve. He was sweating harder than ever.

Brian knew the runner on first was the Mariners' fastest guy. And the next batter was left-handed. Brian might have to make a tough throw if the play came his way.

And suddenly, what he feared was happening. The batter cracked a hard grounder at Jeff Reinhold at second base. The ball skipped by him, and Brian had to charge hard.

He slowed as he approached the ball. He

came in low and under control—just the way Gentel had said to do. Then he scooped the ball up smoothly.

The runner was heading for third, and Brian knew he had to put some real zip on the ball to get him.

He threw with everything he had. But he forced the throw, and the ball took off on him.

It sailed ten feet over Henry's head.

The runner scored, and the batter went to second on the error. Kenny got the side out after that, but the score was now tied.

Brian had missed his chance to drive in a run. And now he had missed his chance to stop one. It was his fault his team wasn't ahead in the game.

It seemed like things just kept getting worse.

Brian walked to the dugout slowly. He didn't want to look at anyone.

But something else was wrong—something besides his discouragement.

His head felt light, almost dizzy, and his knees seemed heavy as he walked. He was really thirsty, but he wasn't going to take a drink—not for anything.

No one said anything to Brian about his bad throw. Jenny yelled, "Come on, you guys, let's get something going. We can't let the Mariners beat us."

But no one seemed excited. Maybe it was the heat. Or maybe everyone believed they were too good to lose to the Mariners.

Coach Wilkens walked over to the dugout. "Look, kids, you better take this team seriously. They're playing a lot better than they did at the start of the season."

Everyone said they were going to get them now, but Brian still didn't think the players were very concerned. But he was. He was going to get a hit this time, *for sure.*

As it turned out, however, he didn't get a chance to bat that inning. The Dodgers were out quickly and back in the field.

Brian jumped up and charged back to right field. But halfway across the outfield, he felt strange again. The heat shimmered in front of him. He couldn't see right.

His head was suddenly aching—throbbing in both temples.

Brian slowed to a walk. But he couldn't focus on anything. Weakness was spreading over him, climbing from his knees into his whole body. He came to a stop, still facing the outfield fence.

"Coach," he heard himself say, and he thought he had yelled. But the word only slipped from his lips.

And then the ground came up and hit his knees, and in another second he was on his chest with grass in his face.

He struggled back to his feet and looked toward the infield, trying to spot the coach. Then he settled to his knees again, too weak to walk off the field.

The coach saw what was happening. "Brian, what's the matter?" he yelled, as he ran toward him.

"I don't know."

The coach knelt by him. "Have you been getting plenty of water into your system?"

Some of the other players were coming up to them.

Brian didn't want to answer.

"Brian, have you been drinking water during the game?"

"No," he whispered.

"Why not?"

"I didn't want to . . . run to the bathroom again."

The coach shook his head slowly. "Oh, Brian, you can't do that. You've let yourself get dehydrated. That's dangerous, son. Really dangerous."

Brian hadn't thought about that. He had only thought about not messing up again.

"Come on, guys," Coach Wilkens said. "Let's get him into the shade."

Some of the players picked Brian up and carried him off the field. But that was the last thing he wanted.

★ 4 ★

Hot Bats

The coach considered sending Brian to the hospital, but there was a doctor in the crowd. He had a look at Brian, who by then was sitting on the grass under a tree. The doctor got some liquid into Brian, and he used a wet towel to cool his head and upper body. He said it was not heat stroke—but it could have been if Brian had gone on much longer.

The coach had Jacob run and call Brian's parents so they could come for him.

Brian was already a lot better, except that he felt like an idiot again. If he wasn't messing up by having to run to the bathroom, now he was messing up by *not* having to.

But Coach Wilkens didn't see it that way.

When the players had carried Brian off the field the whole team had gathered around him.

Danny Sandia had made a crack about "Running" Waters drying up. But the coach hadn't liked that. He spun around and said, "Look, this kid plays his heart out, every game. If all of you would play as hard as he does, we'd have a ten-run lead right now. Most of you are just going through the motions today."

And then he pointed a finger at Danny. "And I'll tell you something else. Brian takes a lot of teasing. And that puts pressure on him. That's one of the reasons he doesn't play as well as he could. If you kids want to be a real team you'll lay off that kind of stuff."

Brian was embarrassed. He didn't want the coach to step in for him that way.

But the players listened to the coach. "Let's go out and kick some butt," Eddie Boschi said. "Let's win it for Brian."

Everyone cheered and ran back to the field.

The weather didn't get any hotter, but the

team sure did. The defense sharpened, and the players' bats caught fire.

Brian wished he could be part of it. He felt pretty good now, but he knew he couldn't go back in the game. One of his parents would be showing up soon. He hoped it was his mom.

The Dodgers' big rally started with Rodney Bunson in the fourth. He hit a shot that whistled past the third baseman and went for a double.

Malone followed with a walk, and then Jenny Roper rapped a line drive that scored Bunson. Sterling went to third.

Jacob came off the bench then and kept his hitting streak alive. He poked a ball into left field and drove in a run. But then Billy Bacon made an out on a foul-ball pop-up. And Harlan Sloan was coming up. It looked like the rally might die.

Brian heard Kenny yell to Harlan, "Come on, keep it going! Drive Jenny home. Remember Brian."

Brian didn't know how he felt about that. He really would rather just be playing—driving in a run himself.

But he was beginning to like the rookies.

They were the ones who understood what it was like to be the "little guys" on the team.

Of course, Harlan was no small fry. He was tall, but he was sort of awkward. Even the hits he got once in a while looked like accidents. But he was like Brian in one way: He always gave the game everything he had.

"Come on, Harlan!" Brian yelled. He knew the coach was right. The whole team had to pull together.

Harlan fouled off a pitch into the dirt. His swing was late.

"Come on, Harlan," Brian yelled again. "Bring those runners home!"

"Just meet the ball," Kenny shouted. "Get the ball in the air. A fly ball will score a run."

Maybe the next pitch was just too fat, or maybe Harlan got lucky. But this time he connected. He drove the ball high and deep.

"All right!" Brian screamed.

The right fielder was going back. If he caught the ball that deep in right, Sterling could walk home from third.

But the fielder just kept going.

All the way to the fence.

And the ball kept right on sailing . . . until it dropped over the fence.

Home run!!!!

Harlan galloped around the bases. He had never learned a home-run trot. But as he rounded third he had a grin on his face that reached both of his big ears.

Brian was happy for him.

Mostly.

Because now he wondered if there was anyone on the team who wasn't playing better than he was.

He wanted to pull together and think mainly of the team. But he also wanted to do his share. He didn't want to be the guy who let everyone else down.

The Dodgers won the game going away. By the time it was over, the score was 14 to 3. Kenny had three hits, and the rookies had all played very well.

Brian was able to watch quite a bit of the game because his parents hadn't been home when Jacob first called.

When Brian's dad finally did get to the park he was in a business suit. He had said that morning that he would probably be at the office until quite late.

"Brian, are you all right?" he asked.

At least he seemed concerned. "Yeah. I just got a little sick there for a minute. I guess it was the heat."

"The kid who called me said you didn't drink so you wouldn't have to go to the bathroom."

Brian didn't say anything. He looked away from his dad.

Mr. Waters didn't kneel down, didn't touch Brian. He stood with his hands in his pockets. He was a small man who always looked neat. He was friendly, in his way, but he usually didn't have much to say to Brian.

"What's this all about?" he said, and he sounded impatient.

"I didn't want to have to run off during the game."

His dad hadn't been to any of the games this year. He didn't know about Brian's dashes to the men's room.

"For heaven's sake, Brian, it's over a hundred degrees today. You ought to know you have to put water into your system when you're out there sweating like that."

Brian nodded.

"Well, come on. Let's get you home."

But just then the coach walked over. "Mr. Waters, that's a fine son you have. He may let himself get a little too uptight, but he plays all out. I guess he told you how he ran into the fence the other night, trying to get to a ball."

"I saw his face," Mr. Waters said. "Brian didn't tell me exactly how it happened." He seemed to think for a few seconds, and then he added, "I guess I don't believe baseball's important enough to get injured over . . . the way you seem to."

Brian knew his dad was on the edge of losing his temper.

"No, I didn't mean that," Coach Wilkens said. "I don't want any of the kids to get hurt—and I sure don't want them getting dehydrated. But I'm just impressed that Brian works so hard to do his best."

Brian hoped his dad might give him a look—maybe show some pride in what the coach had said.

But Mr. Waters shook his head. "Well, I'll tell you, Coach. If I had my way, the boy wouldn't waste his time on sports. He's never going to be that good. He's just too small."

"Actually, he plays very well."

"Maybe. But I bought him a computer, and I think he ought to put more time in on that—or on his violin. Too many people encourage their kids to give all their effort to sports—instead of something that might be more useful in the long run."

"You have the wrong idea if you think the only thing I care about is sports," Coach Wilkens said.

But Mr. Waters wasn't listening. "Come on, son, we need to get you home and out of this heat."

Brian got up and walked away with his dad. Some of the guys from the team yelled to him that they hoped he was okay. Brian waved to them, but he didn't say anything.

He was just hoping he could still be in the starting lineup for the big game.

BOX SCORE, GAME 9

Angel Park Dodgers   14   San Lorenzo Mariners   3

	ab	r	h	rbi		ab	r	h	rbi
White 3b	4	2	3	1	Cast cf	3	0	1	0
Boschi lf	3	0	1	1	Smagler 2b	1	0	0	0
Sandoval p	5	2	3	4	St. Mary lf	2	0	0	0
Bunson ss	4	2	3	2	Antonangeli c	1	0	0	0
Malone cf	3	1	1	0	Watson ss	2	1	1	1
Roper 1b	5	2	3	2	Rodriguez 1b	3	0	1	0
Reinhold 2b	2	1	1	0	Sullivan p	2	0	0	0
Bacon c	4	0	2	0	Cisco 3b	2	0	0	0
Waters rf	1	0	0	0	Tomas rf	3	0	0	0
Sloan rf	3	2	1	3	Korman c	2	1	1	0
Scott 2b	3	1	1	1	Amey lf	0	1	0	0
Sandia lf	3	1	1	0	Perez 2b	1	0	0	0
ttl	**40**	**14**	**20**	**14**		**22**	**3**	**4**	**1**

Dodgers   0 1 0 8 5 0—14
Mariners 0 1 0 0 0 2—3

★ 5 ★

Compromise

Coach Wilkens was sitting in Brian's living room. He had come to see how Brian was doing.

But maybe that had been a mistake. Mr. Waters had only used the chance to announce that it was time for Brian to give up baseball.

"I've thought about it since he got sick last night, and I just don't think it's worth it. He's small, and so he tries to make up for it. It's too much pressure on him."

"But it means so much to him," Mrs. Waters said. She was sitting next to Brian on the fancy white sofa, and she put her arm around him.

"Other things can mean just as much. He

just hasn't given the same effort to anything else."

This debate had been going on since the night before. Brian felt as though he was in a tennis match—and he was the ball.

Twaaannnnggg. Twaaannnnggg.

Coach Wilkens was holding his baseball cap, sitting on the edge of his chair. He looked uncomfortable. "Brian," he said, "your dad has a good point. If baseball isn't fun for you, maybe you shouldn't play. Is that how you feel?"

"No. I want to play," Brian said.

Mr. Waters stood up. "Well, Mr. Wilkens, that's something for Brian and me to talk about. I appreciate your dropping by."

Coach Wilkens stood up, and so did Mrs. Waters. "Coach, you've done a wonderful job with the kids," she said. "They all think a lot of you."

When Mr. Waters offered his hand Coach Wilkens shook it, but he didn't leave. "I'd hate to see Brian quit right now," he said. "We have a good shot at the championship. That would be lots of fun for him. That's what I really care about—that the kids have a good time."

"I don't think he was having a good time when he collapsed last night."

"Mr. Waters," the coach said, "I know you don't think baseball is very important. And I'll agree that it's just a game. But if you love something, and you work hard at it, it's satisfying—and it's also a chance to learn some things about yourself."

"Dad," Brian said, "I don't want to quit until I see how good I can really be."

"Richard," Mrs. Waters said, "it wouldn't be fair to make him quit now—not in the middle of the best season the team has had."

"Look," Mr. Waters said, "I've never tried to interfere before. But I don't see where all the fun is when the game is making him so nervous and worried he can hardly play."

"Maybe he could play when things aren't so tense," Mrs. Waters said. "Coach, couldn't you let him play when you already have a good lead?"

"Well, maybe, but—"

"I want to be a starter, Mom. I want to play as much as I can." But Brian was looking at his dad, and his dad was thinking things over.

"I'm willing to compromise that far," he

said to Brian. "Would you agree to play only at times when you wouldn't have a lot of pressure?"

"The rules say every player must play in every game," Coach Wilkens said.

"Well, some games, you might have to tell the umpire he's sick. And that will be true. I don't want him to play in the championship game at all. He'll be a wreck if he does."

"Dad, I *want* to play in that game."

"Well, take your choice. Either agree to this compromise or don't play at all."

So that was that.

But Brian was not happy with Dad's "compromise."

On Saturday morning Brian put on his uniform and walked to the park, the same as every Saturday. But he didn't expect to play. This game with the Cactus Hills Reds was the biggest of the season so far—and it was bound to be close all the way.

Brian's mom and dad said they were coming. Mom said it was because they wanted to see the big game, but Brian thought that Dad wanted to make sure Brian didn't play.

Brian warmed up with the team. By game time the bleachers were filled, and people were sitting on lawn chairs down the sidelines and even beyond the outfield fences. It was the biggest crowd of the year.

More than half the fans were wearing red. The Cactus Hills supporters had all driven over for the game, and they were making lots of noise already.

Brian went to the bench with the rest of the players, since the Dodgers were batting first. But he was only there to watch. Jacob Scott was playing in right field in his place, and Jacob was excited.

"Ladies and gentlemen," Jacob announced to everyone in the dugout, "this is the big game. This one's for all the marbles. Which is strange. Since no one is playing marbles."

And then he said in his other radio announcer's voice, "Well, it couldn't be for all the baseballs. I guess that's why it's for the marbles. But I don't know why anyone would want marbles when he's playing baseball. It's all very strange."

"Forget the marbles. It's for *blood*," Billy Bacon yelled. "I want some of that *Red* blood. Just give me a chance to slide into that loudmouth third baseman, and I'll come in with my cleats in his face."

But Coach Wilkens heard that one. "Hey, Billy, none of that talk. We're going to be good sports today—no matter how the *Reds* act."

"They act like jerks," Billy mumbled. "Except they don't have to *act*. They *are* jerks."

But just then Jacob said, "He's *here*. He said he might come, but I didn't believe he would do it."

Brian got up and looked around. Kenny's parents were walking across the park, carrying their lawn chairs, but . . . it was him.

Gary Gentel!

When he saw the Dodgers looking at him, Gentel waved, and then he walked toward the dugout.

"Are you kids ready?" he asked them.

"Yeah!" the players all shouted.

"Well, all right. I told Jacob I'd try to make it over and see the *other* Dodgers win the big one—so let's see you play some great baseball."

The Dodgers were psyched, but now lots of other people had seen who was there. Suddenly kids were bailing out of the bleachers, and everyone in the park was standing and stretching to see what all the fuss was about.

The name Gary Gentel spread through the crowd like a wave.

Before sixty seconds had passed, the poor guy had a mob around him. He signed autographs until the game was supposed to start, but even then nothing happened, since both umpires were over trying to get a good look at the Dodger hero.

The home plate umpire, a young man with a crew cut, even got Gentel's autograph himself before he came back and announced it was time to play ball.

Brian watched Gentel. He had to beg the crowd around him to let him sit down. Brian thought it must be great to be that big a hero.

Now he felt even worse that he had to sit on the sidelines and wouldn't have a chance to help his team win—and maybe show the big star that he really could play.

★ 6 ★

Big Game

One thing soon became clear: This game was going to be tight. Both pitchers were looking good. Bunson was firing hard, and he was throwing strikes—but so was Manny Tovar for the Reds.

The game was also what Brian's dad thought it would be: tense.

The Reds' players never missed a chance to upset the Dodgers. They especially liked to work on the rookies.

But the best fun was kept for Brian. Even though he wasn't playing, the Reds started early.

"Hey, Waters, are you ready to do some running? Not around the bases, of course."

"Yeah, he makes a lot of runs for his team—to the john."

Billy yelled back, "Hey, you guys are going to get the runs today—but I'm not talking about *scoring*."

That only kept the insults bouncing back and forth.

Brian stayed out of it, even though he was boiling inside. He wished he could do something to shut them up.

In the second inning the Reds' huge catcher, a guy named Winter, got hold of one of Bunson's fastballs and drove it into the left-center gap for a double. The Reds' fans went nuts.

Winter strutted around. He took off his batting gloves and stuffed them in his back pocket, and he adjusted his red headband. Then he shouted, "You used up all your stuff in the first inning, Bunson! That pitch had nothing on it."

He looked over at Kenny. "Hey, little kid, did your daddy say you could come to the park this morning?"

Kenny smiled, looking friendly. "Yup, he let me come," he said.

That really shut Winter up.

Brian was amazed. He was amazed that Kenny could keep his cool with so many guys on his back.

The batter was Mendelsohn, the center fielder. He wasn't as mouthy as most of the Reds, but he was a good hitter. He let a couple of pitches go by, and then he grounded a ball to the right side.

Jeff had to charge the slow roller, but he made a good play and threw the runner out.

Winter moved to third on the play.

"I'm going home, Bunson," he yelled. "Just watch me!" And then he turned to Kenny. "If it comes to you, I hope you can make a good throw, because I'm *fast,* and I'm going to *go for it.*"

Kenny nodded, as if to say, "Take your shot."

But as it turned out, the ball went the other way. Manny surprised everyone when he put down a perfect bunt along the first-base line. He was safe, and the run scored.

Winter did a lot of yelling about it, too.

The Reds were acting big. The Dodgers were getting tired of listening to them.

Bunson got the side out, and in the third inning Henry White got a single and stole second. Sterling struck out, but Kenny came up to bat.

Brian knew how much Kenny wanted to get a hit. He wondered if the Reds were beginning to get to him.

And the Reds kept pouring it on.

The catcher called to Manny, "He's only a child. Don't hurt the poor little guy."

But Kenny looked calm and even sort of happy. He was smiling a little.

Maybe he was already thinking how much fun it was going to be to get a hit.

And he got it.

He waited for the right pitch and then swung easy and . . . *punch!!* . . . the ball looped into right field.

Henry scored ahead of the right fielder's throw.

Kenny sprinted to first, rounded the base, and then, when the fielder threw home, took the chance to blast over to second.

When the play was over, Kenny was standing on second base. He was smiling a little more than he had before.

The Reds weren't saying much.

Brian wished that he could be like Kenny. He wondered where Sandoval had learned that kind of confidence in himself.

But the Dodgers got nothing more in the inning. The score was tied going into the fourth—still just 1 to 1.

The tension was getting to both teams.

The Dodgers were unusually nervous, Brian thought. They were playing well in the field, but they weren't swinging well against Manny.

The Reds were doing no better, and they seemed to be getting even more uptight. Jimmy Gerstein, the cocky kid who played third, yelled at Bunson, telling him what a rag-arm he was, and the catcher never shut up.

"No one's going to hit Manny," he kept shouting. "You guys might as well not come up to bat."

Brian had never stopped watching Gary Gentel. He seemed to be enjoying himself. Between innings a lot of people collected around his lawn chair near the first-base line.

But as soon as the batter stepped in to

start the next inning, he would ask the kids to wait so he could watch.

He didn't seem to mind all the attention.

Brian thought again it would be nice to be so famous.

In fact, Brian was working on a pretty good daydream. The coach would decide to put him in after all. Brian would knock out hits every time up and catch everything that came his way.

Then he would talk his dad into letting him play in all the games. He'd drive in the winning run for the championship, and he'd make the all-star team. He'd go on to high school ball and then the minors, and someday . . .

But Brian stopped himself. He would settle for just being one of the solid players on the team—someone no one laughed at. He didn't have to be a superstar.

In the bottom of the fourth inning Mendelsohn hit a ground ball that Harlan probably should have handled at first. But it was hit hard, and Harlan let it bounce off his glove.

The runner would have stopped at first

base, but Jacob hurried his throw to first. The ball was over Harlan's head, and the runner trotted on to second.

"He's supposed to hold the ball and run straight at the runner until the guy commits to go one way or the other," Brian said to Jenny. "That's what the coach always taught me."

"I know," Jenny said. "But he's just learning. That's why we need someone like you out there. You've got more experience."

Brian believed that. For a moment he really thought he might ask the coach if he could play after all, no matter what his parents would say.

Tovar was coming up again. Brian didn't want to see the game lost just because the rookies weren't ready to handle such a tough situation.

But then Kenny made a leaping stab to catch Tovar's line drive, and he flipped the ball to Jeff to double off the runner.

Maybe they could do it without Brian. Especially with a rookie like Kenny.

And in the top of the fifth things started looking even better.

Jenny went back in for Harlan, and she worked Manny for a walk—only the second one of the game.

Then Danny Sandia bounced a grounder at the third baseman. Gerstein threw to first, but the ball hit the dirt and everyone was safe.

Gerstein turned his smart mouth on himself, screaming and swearing, and then he started kicking at the bag.

It seemed the right time to break the game open. Billy was coming up. And the Reds were losing their cool.

Billy turned to the players in the dugout and said, "I'm sick of these guys' big mouths. I'm going to show them what I can do."

Sure enough, that huge catcher Winter started in as soon as Billy walked to the plate.

"Hey, Pork," he said. "Don't let Manny scare you. Just stay way back from the plate—since you don't move too fast."

Brian heard Billy say, "Catch the ball with your mouth, Winter."

The umpire told the boys to lay off, but Brian could see that they kept mumbling to each other.

At least they did until Billy crunched Manny's fastball.

The center fielder charged and held Billy to a single, and only one run scored. But now the Dodgers had the lead.

And that's how things stayed into the bottom of the inning. The Dodgers had their chance now—they just had to hold on.

Brian was excited. The first-half championship was only six outs away.

But . . . he wanted to be part of this. And he had been thinking of a way.

He just wasn't sure he had the guts to try it.

★ 7 ★

Hold Everything!

=================================

"Coach, I want to play."

"What?" Coach Wilkens looked surprised. "Brian, you know I can't put you in now."

"Why not?" Brian grinned. "We've broken the game open. We've got a *big* lead."

"Oh, sure."

"Really. We've got a lead, and Bunson can hold it. But I'm a better defensive player than Jacob. I ought to be out there."

"Don't think I haven't been thinking that. But you know what your dad said."

"I'll show him I can handle it."

"No, I don't think—"

"Come on, Coach. I'm not even on the team if I only play when we've already won the games."

"I know, Brian. I didn't like this whole deal in the first place. But that's what you agreed to. Besides, I told the ump before the game that you had gotten sick in the last game and your parents had asked that you not play in this one."

"Tell him I'm okay now. I can still play six outs, and I can still bat once. That's the rule."

"Your dad will never let you play again *ever* if I do that."

Brian thought about it. "Okay, I'll take that chance," he finally said. "If you'll let me play I'll either show him I can do it or I'll quit baseball."

"Come on, Brian. You don't need that kind of pressure. Why don't we just keep it the way we left it before?"

"Coach, I want to be a baseball player. I can't be one unless I can handle the hard stuff."

Coach Wilkens shook his head, but he was smiling. "Well, okay. I guess I'll take the heat from your dad, but you gotta know, this might be your last game."

"Yeah, I know. It's all or nothing."

So the coach went to talk to the umpire, and Brian trotted out to right field. By the time the coach was walking back and the batter was stepping to the plate, Mr. Waters was leaning against the fence, yelling, "Coach Wilkens, I want to talk to you!"

The coach looked his way and yelled back, "We're about to start the inning. I'll talk to you later, all right?" He kept walking down the first-base line toward the dugout.

Mr. Waters followed.

Brian couldn't hear what the two said after that, but he was sure his father was demanding that he not play, and he could see that the coach wasn't giving in.

Gerstein led off and hit a pop-up that looked as if it was heading for right field. Brian started in—his stomach suddenly tight. But Jeff Reinhold drifted back from his position at second and made the catch.

Brian slumped back with relief. And yet, he almost wished the ball had come to him.

He couldn't prove anything unless he made some plays.

His dad was still talking, and the coach looked back once in a while. But he wasn't waving Brian in.

Finally his dad spun on his heels and walked away.

Brian could see how angry he was. Everything was on the line now. Maybe he never should have gotten himself into this situation.

No. He was going to do it. He knew he could.

Brian waited as the batter fouled off a couple of pitches and then watched Bunson throw a hard fastball for a third strike. "Way to go, Rodney!" he yelled.

Jeff turned around and called out, "Two away." He held up two fingers, like horns.

Four outs to go. Brian *wanted* the next one . . . and he also *didn't* want it. His hands were shaking and his breathing came short and fast.

The batter grounded the ball straight to Jenny. Brian charged in to cover in case the ball got through. But that wasn't necessary. Jenny picked it up and stepped on the bag.

Brian trotted into the dugout. He would be batting first.

"What did my dad say?" he asked the coach.

Coach Wilkens was heading for the coach's box on the first-base side, not far from the dugout. "He didn't think I should put you in."

"I know. But what did you tell him?"

"I said it was your choice. I let you decide for yourself, and I thought he ought to leave it up to you, too."

"Do you think he'll let me play anymore after this?"

Brian saw the coach hesitate. "Brian, you'll have to talk to him and see what you can work out."

Brian knew what that meant. He had to do something to prove he could handle the situation.

And right now it meant getting a hit. He took some long, deep breaths before he stepped to the plate. "No pressure," he told himself. "No one on base. We've got the lead."

But he could feel his dad watching.

And that was pressure.

Brian swung at the first pitch—a ball down and away, out of the strike zone. It was a stupid pitch to swing at.

And so he held up on the next pitch . . . and took a strike down the middle.

Why did he do things like that? He was a *good* hitter in practice, when he just forgot about everything and took his best swing.

But he swung hard again at a pitch that was outside. Manny had suckered him, and he had gone for it.

Brian tossed the bat away and trudged back to the dugout.

But he was not there long. Henry and Sterling had no luck at bat either.

The important thing now was that the team get three outs and win the first-half championship. But if he didn't do something right in the sixth inning . . .

He would. He had to.

Bunson was still firing hard. Schulman, the left fielder, was up first. All the Dodgers were shouting to Bunson to mow him down.

That only brought on more yelling from the other side. Everyone knew this was it—three outs—and the noise was building with every pitch.

Bunson put a beautiful pitch on the inside corner of the plate. Schulman complained about it being inside, but the ump told him to turn around and play ball. The next pitch was a little outside, and Schulman didn't go for it.

He was playing it smarter than Brian had. But he couldn't match Bunson's heat. He swung and missed on a hard, low fastball.

"Put one more by him, Bunson!" Brian shouted.

And Bunson came through. He fired what looked like his hardest pitch of the day. Schulman swung and missed by a foot.

The Dodgers all cheered, and so did their fans. And then—immediately—the tension set back in.

One down. Two to go.

Brian wanted at least one of them. He had to do something right.

Winter, the big catcher, was coming up. Brian knew how great it would feel to make a good catch on him.

Winter took a ball outside, and then he hit a pitch on the nose. It skittered past Jeff Reinhold and into right field. Brian charged toward the ball.

He wanted to hold Winter to a single, and so he came at the ball fast—maybe too fast.

It took a low hop, slipped under his glove, and rolled behind him.

He only had to backtrack a few steps, and then he grabbed the ball and gunned it to Kenny at second. But it was too late. Winter had used the chance to take the extra base.

Now the runner was in scoring position. And Brian had messed up again.

"What's the matter, Waters?" Winter yelled. "Do you need to make a little trip?"

Brian acted as though he hadn't heard a thing.

But his stomach was sick.

★ 8 ★

Big Star, Little Star

Maybe it didn't matter.

Maybe Brian should just quit baseball and do what his dad said: find something else, something he was better at.

It wasn't fun to feel this sick and this scared.

But Brian also knew he could play the game. Why couldn't he play it when he had to?

"I'm going to now," he told himself. "Just give me another chance, Reds."

But Bunson was trying to do it by himself. Mendelsohn, the Reds' center fielder, was up again, and Bunson was going after him.

He got the first pitch up too high, but then he came in with a firecracker of a fastball that left Mendelsohn standing there.

The Dodgers' fielders were talking it up, keeping the pressure on the batter, and firing up Bunson.

Everyone in the crowd was screaming, too.

Bunson used his big motion but did a change-up with the ball. It floated in slowly, and Mendelsohn swung way too early. He squibbed the ball off the end of the bat right back to Bunson.

Bunson spun around and looked the runner back to second, and then he threw to Jenny for the out.

Two away. It all came down to one out.

Maybe Brian had muffed his one chance. Dad was probably waiting to tell him he had played his last game.

But Tovar was coming up. He could hit the ball a long way. Brian still might get another shot.

Or maybe he didn't want it.

Everyone was going nuts. All the Reds were standing up in the dugout, screaming at Tovar that he had to bring the run home. And all the Dodgers were yelling to Bunson to strike him out.

And then Tovar swung.

He laced a line drive straight at Brian.

It was low and hard, and Brian had to hurry.

He charged the ball, but it was dropping fast. For an instant Brian didn't know whether to dive or to let it take a bounce.

And in that instant he ended up doing neither. He stuck his glove down but didn't really go after the ball enough to catch it.

The ball bounced just in front of his glove and then hit him in the stomach. He was on it quickly, however, and he fired hard to Billy at home plate. The runner had to stop at third.

Brian slammed his fist into his glove. Why hadn't he gone for it? Maybe he could have made the catch and won the game.

"Good job!" Kenny yelled. "You kept the run from scoring. We'll get this next guy."

That's what everyone was saying, but Brian wasn't sure what they were thinking.

He turned around and walked back to his position. He no longer had any hopes of being the star. He just wanted the team to win. And then he would quit.

When Brian turned back toward the infield he saw the Reds' coach calling the batter back. He sent out a new batter, putting the first baseman who had started the game back in.

He was left-handed.

Brian knew exactly what their coach was thinking. A left-handed batter was more likely to pull the ball to right. And that was the Dodgers' weak spot.

Brian thought maybe he should quit now, not after the game. The coach couldn't take him out, since he hadn't played long enough. But Brian could say he was sick again.

He had to decide right now.

And then he heard someone call "Time out."

It wasn't a coach or a player. It was . . . *Gary Gentel.*

Gentel had called "Time out" just as though he were on the team, and he was walking out toward Brian.

"Hey, he can't do that," the Reds' coach was yelling.

But the umpire shrugged as if to say, "What am I going to do? Kick Gary Gentel off the field?"

Brian didn't know what to do. He just watched the great star trot out to him.

"I need to talk to you for a sec," Gentel said as he reached Brian, and he grinned. He put his hands on his hips and stood with his back to the infield. "I can see that you're letting yourself get awfully upset. You're tight as a fist."

Brian nodded. But he couldn't believe this was happening.

"When I was in Little League, I used to have the same problem. I wanted so bad to be good that I *couldn't* be."

Brian was amazed.

"One time I struck out four times in a game, dropped a couple of fly balls, made three or four bad throws—everything. I almost quit that day."

"That's what I'm going to do."

"No, you can't quit until you do something *really* dumb—like I did one time. I finally got a hit, and I got so excited I ran right past the runner on first and got to second before he did. Then I had to run back to first, and by then they tagged me out—sliding into first the second time I'd been there."

Brian found himself smiling.

"Another time I got so nervous I got a three-and-two count on me and was digging in for the payoff pitch, and all of a sudden I just up and vomited right on home plate."

"Really?"

"Cross my heart." He made a big cross on his chest.

"How did you stop being so nervous?"

"I didn't. I still don't eat before games. I don't want to throw up on home plate . . . on TV."

"You still get nervous?"

"I sure do."

The umpire was walking to the outfield, with the Reds' coach right behind. "Excuse me, Mr. Gentel," the ump was saying.

"Listen, Brian, here's the point. You can't stand out here and tell yourself you're going to mess up. Shut your eyes for a second and picture yourself doing something great. Go ahead."

Brian shut his eyes, but he couldn't think of a thing.

"Say to yourself, 'I can't wait for the ball to come to me, because I'm going to have some fun doing something terrific.' You can't make a great catch unless the ball comes to you. So you hope it does."

"Mr. Gentel, we really need to get going here," the umpire said. He tapped Gentel on the shoulder.

"Okay. We're ready." Gentel grinned at Brian. "Look at it this way—you still haven't vomited on home plate, so you're ahead of me. And if you keep playing, and expecting something good—you'll get to do some great things."

Brian nodded, and Gary Gentel patted him on the head and then walked away.

"Sir, could I get your autograph after the game?" the umpire asked. "The home plate ump got one, and I'd really—"

"Sure. Sure. Come over right after this inning."

The Reds' coach didn't like the delay. He complained all the way back to his coach's box, but the umpire paid no attention.

Brian did his best to make use of the time. He kept shutting his eyes, trying to imagine something really good happening.

The left-handed batter stepped in and took a big swing—and got nothing.

Brian shut his eyes and tried to think what he might have done if the guy had hit the ball. He saw himself running hard and catching a long fly ball.

And then it *was* coming.

The guy hit the next pitch hard. It took off like a shot to Brian's left. It was hit high and long.

Brian ran toward the fence.

He was going all out, seeming to keep up as the ball angled downward. He could get there if . . .

He remembered what had happened before and checked quickly to make sure he had room.

Just before he reached the fence he slowed, and then he jumped—stretched full out.

That fraction of a second seemed like a minute.

He felt the ball sink into the pocket of his glove.

When he came down he had to look just to make sure he really had the ball. He stood there staring at it. And then he looked up to see his whole team charging out toward him.

They were all yelling and screaming, "You did it, Brian! You did it!"

Brian trotted toward them, smiling. Someone grabbed him, and suddenly he was being hoisted up in the air—on the players' shoulders. They ran him all the way back to the infield that way, while the Dodgers' fans in the crowd stood and cheered.

Brian wondered if he still had his eyes closed. Maybe he was just dreaming up all this good stuff.

Gary Gentel was standing on the sideline with both fists raised in the air, yelling, "I knew you could do it, Brian!"

That had to be a dream.

But there was his dad walking toward him across the diamond, smiling and nodding, looking very satisfied. And looking just as *real* as he could be.

It was no dream.

Dad would never let himself get caught in a dream.

Brian had finally done what he always knew he *could* do.

And he felt ready to do *some more*.

BOX SCORE, GAME 10

Angel Park Dodgers 2

	ab	r	h	rbi
White 3b	3	1	1	0
Malone cf	4	0	1	0
Sandoval ss	3	0	1	1
Bunson p	2	0	1	0
Roper 1b	1	1	0	0
Reinhold 2b	2	0	1	0
Bacon c	2	0	1	1
Boschi lf	3	0	0	0
Scott rf	2	0	0	0
Sloan 1b	1	0	0	0
Sandia 2b	0	0	0	0
Waters rf	1	0	0	0
ttl	24	2	6	2

Cactus Hills Reds 1

	ab	r	h	rbi
Gerstein 3b	3	0	0	0
Alfonsi 2b	3	0	0	0
Schulman lf	3	0	1	0
Winter c	3	1	2	0
Mendelsohn cf	3	0	1	0
Tovar p	3	0	2	1
Rutter 1b	2	0	0	0
Trulis rf	0	0	0	0
Young ss	1	0	0	0
Bonthuis 1b	0	0	0	0
Higdon rf	1	0	0	0
Lum ss	1	0	0	0
	23	1	6	1

Dodgers	0	0	1	0	1	0—2
Reds	0	1	0	0	0	0—1

League standings after ten games (first half):

Dodgers	9–1
Reds	8–2
Giants	6–4
Padres	3–7
Mariners	2–8
A's	2–8

Ninth-game scores:

Dodgers	14	Mariners	3
Giants	13	A's	3
Reds	7	Padres	2

Tenth-game scores:

Dodgers	2	Reds	1
Giants	9	Padres	6
A's	6	Mariners	1

DEAN HUGHES has written many books for children including the popular *Nutty* stories and *Jelly's Circus*. He has also published such works of literary fiction for young adults as the highly acclaimed *Family Pose*. When he's not attending Little League games, Mr. Hughes devotes his full time to writing. He lives in Utah with his wife and family.

ANGEL PARK ALL-STARS #1

Making the Team
by Dean Hughes
**They aced the tryouts—but can they win
over their teammates?**

Kenny, Jacob, and Harlan are the three youngest
Little Leaguers to make the Angel Park Dodgers.
They're all anxious to prove themselves to the older
guys, but they haven't counted on the antagonism
of team slugger (and bully!) Rodney Bunson. He'll
do *anything* to stay on top. Can the rookies survive
Rodney's version of hardball? Can the Dodgers?

FIRST TIME IN PRINT!

BULLSEYE BOOKS PUBLISHED BY ALFRED A. KNOPF

ANGEL PARK ALL-STARS #2

Big Base Hit
by Dean Hughes

He really needs one—or he may be off the team!

His buddies Kenny and Jacob (the other third graders on the team) have already gotten their hits. Harlan knows he won't really feel like an Angel Park Dodger until he gets his. But no dice—the harder he tries, the worse it gets. Soon everyone's starting to worry—especially Harlan. What if he never gets a hit? What if he doesn't belong on the team after all?

FIRST TIME IN PRINT!

BULLSEYE BOOKS PUBLISHED BY ALFRED A. KNOPF

ANGEL PARK ALL-STARS #3

Winning Streak
by Dean Hughes
**It's been great so far—but
is their luck finally running out?**

They were hotter than hot the first four games of the season, but now it looks as though Kenny and the Angel Park Dodgers are headed for a slump. The third-grade rookies try all kinds of tricks to change their luck, but when they continue to strike out, zany, brainy Jacob decides to take drastic action. But what if his wild scheme fails? What if he *can't* get the Dodgers back on the winning track?

FIRST TIME IN PRINT!

BULLSEYE BOOKS PUBLISHED BY ALFRED A. KNOPF

The Secret Life of the Underwear Champ

by Betty Miles

**Would you go on network television...
in your underwear?**

Starring in television commercials sure isn't what it's cracked up to be, discovers ten-year-old Larry Pryor. The shooting schedule conflicts with his baseball practice, and he actually has to wear makeup on film! But the biggest problem is what Larry's supposed to be modeling. They can't really expect him to go on TV in his underwear...can they?

"Yay! for a fast-reading book that's sure-fire fun."
—*School Library Journal*

"Thoroughly enjoyable, from start to finish!"
—*The Los Angeles Times*

An IRA-CBC Children's Choice
A Child Study Association Children's Book of the Year
A Georgia Children's Book Award Winner
A Mark Twain Award Winner

BULLSEYE BOOKS PUBLISHED BY ALFRED A. KNOPF

Skinnybones
by Barbara Park
He had the biggest mouth in the Little League!

"I've been in Little League for six years now. But to tell you the truth, I'm not what you'd call a real good athlete. Actually, I'm not even real fair. I'm more what you'd call real stinky."

That's Alex "Skinnybones" Frankovitch for you. For the smallest kid on the baseball team, he's sure got a major-league talent for wisecracking. But even Alex knows he's gone too far when he brags his way into a battle of skills with T. J. Stoner, the Little League legend with a perfect pitching record. What a disaster! This looks like one mess not even Alex can talk his way out of.

"Park is one of the funniest writers around."
—*Booklist*

BULLSEYE BOOKS PUBLISHED BY ALFRED A. KNOPF

Don't Make Me Smile
by Barbara Park
How can they expect him to be happy when they're ruining his life?

The way Charlie Hickle sees it, there's no reason to smile. His parents are getting a divorce, and there doesn't seem to be anything he can do about it. Not that Charlie doesn't try. He does everything he can think of to convince his parents that he'll go nuts if they get a divorce. He threatens to spend the rest of his life in a tree. He refuses to eat his mother's cooking. He causes trouble in school and makes rude comments about his father's new apartment. With a little help from a new friend, though, Charlie finally start to accept the inevitable changes in his life—but not until he makes a hilarious last-ditch effort to get his parents back together.

"Funny and touching—a good read."
—*Children's Book Review Service*

"The author does make you smile, proving that there is still room for one more middle-grade problem novel on divorce."
—*Booklist*

BULLSEYE BOOKS PUBLISHED BY ALFRED A. KNOPF

The Tiny Parents
by Ellen Weiss and Mel Friedman
**Forget about a normal childhood
when your folks are only 2½ inches tall!**

Eddie and Marie Bicker's parents have always been a little...well, unusual. They'll never win any prizes for housekeeping. They squabble constantly. And they spend all their time in their basement laboratory, working on some pretty oddball inventions. But when one of their experiments goes haywire, Mr. and Mrs. Bicker give new meaning to the word *weird*. They start shrinking—and before you can say "Tom Thumb," they're smaller than your average salt shaker. Worse, they've now got the speeded-up metabolisms (and shortened life spans!) of very small creatures. Poor Eddie and Marie. They've got to find a way to get their tiny parents back to life-size soon, or they may find themselves with no parents at all!

FIRST TIME IN PRINT!

BULLSEYE BOOKS PUBLISHED BY ALFRED A. KNOPF

Mystery of the Plumed Serpent
by Barbara Brenner
Something fishy is going on in the pet shop!

At first, twins Elena and Michael are thrilled to see boxes of exotic animals being moved into the empty next door. They can't wait for the pet store to open up. But when it does, their excitement turns into suspicion. The owners aren't very friendly (not even to grownups who might be customers!) and they don't sem to know anything about the animals they're selling. When one of the monkeys drops a piece of gold jewelry into Elena's hand, the twins realize that they're on to something big. Like it or not, they've accidentally broken the cover of a desperate gang of smugglers and their cache of stolen Mexican treasure—and that's double trouble for all concerned!

"Perfect for reluctant as well as regular readers."
—*School Library Journal*

"Fast-paced with lots of action…Highly recommended." —*Catholic Library World*

BULLSEYE BOOKS PUBLISHED BY ALFRED A. KNOPF

Who Stole *The* Wizard *of* Oz?
by Avi
A missing book holds the key to hidden treasure!

Becky is furious! The Checkertown librarian has accused her of stealing a rare children's book, and she's determined to prove her innocence by tracking down the real culprit. With the help of her twin brother, Toby, Becky investigates a rash of other oddball crimes about town—including the disappearance of four more children's books. The twins think they've hit paydirt when they discover that clues to the mystery—directions to a secret treasure—can be found in the stories themselves. But can they piece together their elusive treasure map...before the real thief does?

"Avi combines simplicity of style with wit as he builds a believable, gripping plot that his highly accessible." —*Booklist*

"This is fun reading!" —*School Library Journal*

BULLSEYE BOOKS PUBLISHED BY ALFRED A. KNOPF

ENTER THE ANGEL PARK ALL-STARS SWEEPSTAKES!

- The Grand Prize: a trip for four to the 1991 All-Star Game in Toronto
- 25 First Prizes: Louisville Slugger Little League bat personalized with the winner's name and the Angel Park All-Stars logo

See official entry rules below.

OFFICIAL RULES—NO PURCHASE NECESSARY

1. On an official entry form print your name, address, zip code, age, and the answer to the following question: What are the names of the three main characters in the Angel Park All-Stars books? The information needed to answer this question can be found in any of the Angel Park All-Stars books, or you may obtain an entry form, a set of rules, and the answer to the question by writing to: Angel Park Request, P.O. Box 3352, Syosset, NY 11775-3352. Each request must be mailed separately and must be received by November 1, 1990.

2. Enter as often as you wish, but each entry must be mailed separately to: ANGEL PARK ALL-STARS SWEEPSTAKES, P.O. Box 3335, Syosset, NY 11775-3335. No mechanically reproduced entries will be accepted. All entries must be received by December 1, 1990.

3. **Winners will be selected, from among correct entries received, in a random drawing conducted by National Judging Institute, Inc., an independent judging organization whose decisions are final on all matters relating to this sweepstakes. All prizes will be awarded and winners notified by mail. Prizes are nontransferable, and no substitutions or cash equivalents are allowed. Taxes, if any, are the responsibility of the individual winners. Winners may be asked to verify address or execute an affidavit of eligibility and release. No responsibility is assumed for lost, misdirected, or late entries or mail. Grand Prize consists of a three-day/two-night trip for a family of four to the 1991 All-Star Game in Toronto, Canada, including round-trip air transportation, hotel accommodations, game tickets, hotel-to-airport and hotel-to-game transfers, and breakfasts and dinners. In the event the trip is won by a minor, it will be awarded in the name of a parent or legal guardian. Trip must be taken on date specified or the prize will be forfeited and an alternate winner selected. RANDOM HOUSE, INC., and its affiliates reserve the right to use the prize winners' names and likenesses in any promotional activities relating to this sweepstakes without further compensation to the winners.**

4. Sweepstakes open to residents of the U.S. and Canada, except for the Province of Quebec. Employees and their families of RANDOM HOUSE, INC., and its affiliates, subsidiaries, advertising agencies, and retailers, and Don Jagoda Associates, Inc., may not enter. This offer is void wherever prohibited, and subject to all federal, state, and local laws.

5. **For a list of winners, send a stamped, self-addressed envelope to: ANGEL PARK WINNERS, P.O. Box 3347, Syosset, NY 11775-3347.**

Angel Park All-Stars Sweepstakes Official Entry Form

Name:_____ Age:_____
(Please Print)

Address_____

City/State/Zip:_____

What are the names of the three main characters in the Angel Park All-Stars books?

_____